Margaret Hillert's

What Am I?

xz
IR
H

A Beginning-to-Read Book

Illustrated by Lucy Makuc

DEAR CAREGIVER,

The books in this Beginning-to-Read collection may look somewhat familiar in that the original versions could have been a part of your own early reading experiences. These carefully written texts feature common sight words to provide your child multiple exposures to the words appearing most frequently in written text. These new versions have been updated and the engaging illustrations are highly appealing to a contemporary audience of young readers.

Begin by reading the story to your child, followed by letting him or her read familiar words and soon your child will be able to read the story independently. At each step of the way, be sure to praise your reader's efforts to build his or her confidence as an independent reader. Discuss the pictures and encourage your child to make connections between the story and his or her own life. At the end of the story, you will find reading activities and a word list that will help your child practice and strengthen beginning reading skills. These activities, along with the comprehension questions are aligned to current standards, so reading efforts at home will directly support the instructional goals in the classroom.

Above all, the most important part of the reading experience is to have fun and enjoy it!

Shannon Cannon

Shannon Cannon,
Literacy Consultant

Norwood House Press • www.norwoodhousepress.com
Beginning-to-Read™ is a registered trademark of Norwood House Press.
Illustration and cover design copyright ©2017 by Norwood House Press. All Rights Reserved.

Authorized adapted reprint from the U.S. English language edition, entitled What Am I? by Margaret Hillert. Copyright © 2017 Margaret Hillert. Reprinted with permission. All rights reserved. Pearson and What Am I? are trademarks, in the US and/or other countries, of Pearson Education, Inc. or its affiliates. This publication is protected by copyright, and prior permission to re-use in any way in any format is required by both Norwood House Press and Pearson Education. This book is authorized in the United States for use in schools and public libraries.

Designer: Lindaanne Donohoe
Editorial Production: Lisa Walsh

LIBRARY OF CONGRESS CATALOGING-IN-PUBLICATION DATA
Names: Hillert, Margaret, author. | Makuc, Lucy, illustrator.
Title: What am I? / by Margaret Hillert ; illustrated by Lucy Makuc.
Description: Chicago, IL : Norwood House Press, [2016] | Series: A beginning-to-read book
Identifiers: LCCN 2016001862 (print) | LCCN 2016024348 (ebook) | ISBN 9781599538204 (library edition : alk. paper) | ISBN 9781603579919 (eBook)
Subjects: LCSH: Riddles, Juvenile.
Classification: LCC PN6371.5 .H5 2016 (print) | LCC PN6371.5 (ebook) | DDC 818/.5402—dc23
LC record available at https://lccn.loc.gov/2016001862

I am big.
I can go, go, go.
You can ride in me.
What am I?

A car.
A car to ride in.

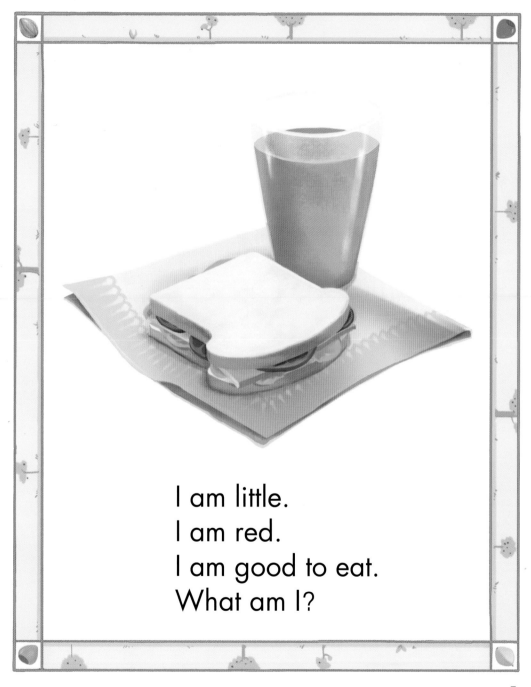

I am little.
I am red.
I am good to eat.
What am I?

An apple.
A good red apple.

I am little.
I can jump, jump, jump.
You like little me.
What am I?

A rabbit.
A rabbit that can jump.

Up and down.
Up and down.
I can go up.
I can come down.
I am fun to play with.
What am I?

A swing.
A swing that goes up and down.

I am blue.
I am up, up, up.
You have to look up
to see me.
What am I?

The sky.
The blue, blue sky.

I am not in the house.
I am out.
I am green.
I get big, big, big.
What am I?

A tree.
A big, big tree.

I run with you.
I jump with you.
I look like you.
What am I?

A shadow.
A shadow that looks like you.

I am yellow.
I look good.
You can eat me.
What am I?

A banana.
A banana to eat.

I am big.
I can jump, jump, jump.
My baby is with me.
What am I?

A kangaroo.
A mother kangaroo with a baby.

You can go up.
You can go down.
This is fun for you to do.
What am I?

A slide.
A slide for you to
go up and down.

I come down.
Down, down, down.
I make you run
but you like me.
What am I?

Rain.
Rain to play in.

I can not run.
I can not jump.
I am too little.
My mother helps me.
What am I?

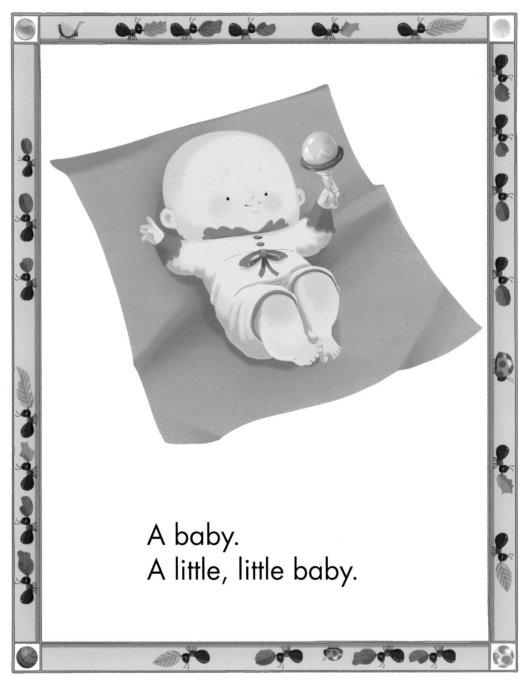

A baby.
A little, little baby.

I go up, up, up.
Away and away.
You ride in me.
What am I?

An airplane.
An airplane that goes up—
and away!

Foundational Skills

In addition to reading the numerous high-frequency words in the text, this book also supports the development of foundational skills.

Phonological Awareness: The diphthong /ou/ (spelled ow)

Oral Blending: Say the beginning sounds and word endings below for your child. Some words also have a middle sound. Say each word part separately. Ask your child to say the new word made by blending the beginning, middle and ending word parts together:

/n/ + ow = now   /b/ + ow = bow
/t/ + ow + /n/ = town   /cl/ + ow + /n/ = clown
/f/ + ow + /l/ = fowl   /h/ + ow = how
/ch/ + ow = chow   /br/ + ow + /n/ = brown
/d/ + ow + /n/ = down   /c/ + ow = cow
/pl/ + ow = plow   /fr/ + ow + /n/ = frown

Phonics: The letters o and w

1. Demonstrate how to form the letters **o** and **w** for your child.
2. Have your child practice writing **o** and **w** at least three times each.
3. Write down the following words, with spaces, and ask your child to complete each word by adding the letters **o** and **w** in the spaces:

n__ __   h__ __   cr__ __ n   t__ __ n   ch__ __
h__ __ l   pl__ __   s__ __   d__ __ n   cl__ __ n
b__ __   v__ __   g__ __n   gr__ __l   t__ __er

4. Ask your child to read each word.

Fluency: Echo Reading

1. Reread the story to your child at least two more times while your child tracks the print by running a finger under the words as they are read. Ask your child to read the words he or she knows with you.
2. Reread the story, stopping after each sentence or page to allow your child to read (echo) what you have read. Repeat echo reading and let your child take the lead.

Language

The concepts, illustrations, and text help children develop language both explicitly and implicitly.

Vocabulary: Adjectives

1. Explain to your child that words that describe something are called adjectives.
2. Write the following adjectives from the story on index cards and ask your child to read them and name something they might describe:

big	red	little	fun
green	yellow	big	blue

3. After reading the story, provide your child with additional index cards with the nouns from the story and help him/her match the adjective with the appropriate noun:

car	apple	rabbit	swing
tree	banana	kangaroo	sky

Reading Literature and Informational Text

To support comprehension, ask your child the following questions. The answers either come directly from the text or require inferences and discussion.

Key Ideas and Detail

- Ask your child to retell the riddles in the story.
- What are the things you can eat in the book?

Craft and Structure

- Is this a book that tells a story or one that gives information? How do you know?
- What are your favorite riddles in the book?

Integration of Knowledge and Ideas

- What other things beside a bunny could the riddle on page 7 be about?
- Can you make your own riddles?

What Am I? uses the 64 words listed below.

This list can be used to practice reading the words that appear in the text. You may wish to write the words on index cards and use them to help your child build automatic word recognition. Regular practice with these words will enhance your child's fluency in reading connected text.

a	do	I	not	that
airplane	down	in		the
am		is	out	this
an	eat			to
and		jump	play	too
apple	for			tree
away	fun	kangaroo	rabbit	
			rain	up
baby	get	like	red	
banana	go	little	ride	what
big	goes	look (ɔ)	run	with
blue	good			
but	green	make	see	yellow
		me	shadow	you
can	have	mother	sky	
car	helps	my	slide	
come	house		swing	

ABOUT THE AUTHOR Margaret Hillert has helped millions of children all over the world learn to read independently. She was a first grade teacher for 34 years and during that time started writing books that her students could both gain confidence in reading and enjoy. She wrote well over 100 books for children just learning to read. As a child, she enjoyed writing poetry and continued her poetic writings as an adult for both children and adults.

Photograph by Glenna Washburn

ABOUT THE ILLUSTRATOR Lucy Makuc was born in Argentina. She studied at the National Institute of Art of Argentina. After, she continued to study in many other places, with the goal of growing as an artist. Now she works as an illustrator and comic artist for many publishers. In her free time, she enjoys gardening, playing with her cats, and making new projects with her husband, who is also an illustrator.